Ahmed's Journey

Acknowledgments

Thank you to the people of Saudi Arabia for sharing your culture and country with me.
May *Ahmed's Journey* continue to inspire children everywhere.

Dedication

... to my children, Christina, Dana, John, and Ron

... to children everywhere

Published by
JABU BOOKS ~ NEWPORT BEACH, CA

Publisher's Cataloging-in-Publication Data
Manly, Jill Apperson.
Ahmed's journey : a story of self-discovery / Jill Apperson Manly. – Newport Beach, CA : Jabu Bks., 2018.

p. ; cm.

ISBN13: 978-0-9980220-0-0

1. Children--Juvenile fiction. 2. Self-perception--Juvenile fiction. 3. Travel--Juvenile fiction. I. Title.
PZ7.1.M36 2018
[E]--dc23 2018904407

Photoshop by Iyesha van den Haak
Design by Yvonne Fetig Roehler

Printed in the United States of America by Bang Printing, First Printing, June 2018
22 21 20 19 18 • 5 4 3 2 1

Ahmed's Journey

A Story of Self-Discovery

Jill Apperson Manly

Jabu Books ~ Newport Beach, CA

Ahmed lives in the

Arabian Peninsula,

where *drifting*

sand dunes form

VAST

deserts.

Camels roam free,

and families

enjoy sipping

hot sweet tea.

Tomorrow will be a special day for Ahmed. He and his family have crossed the desert to race their camels in the famous camel races.

The journey to bring the family and their camels across the desert was l o n g and hot. Setting up camp offered relief and comfort to everyone.

As the sun heats the land, Ahmed joins his father and brothers in the shade. He listens to their laughter as they share stories of past races, but Ahmed does not feel excited like the others.

Instead, he feels

small,

sad,

and lonely.

After a time,

Ahmed leaves the tent

and goes to feed the camels.

Saving Jamal, his favorite camel,

for last, Ahmed rubs Jamal's ear

and gives him extra food.

It is quiet

away from the camp

and the lively chatter

of Ahmed's family.

In the silence,

Ahmed observes the camels

and the other desert animals.

A golden spiny mouse eats
a small bit of Jamal's meal.

A
Saker falcon perches
in a
lone
tree.

Ahmed squints into the distance

and sees a sandstorm forming.

The wind is *strengthening*,

picking up millions of grains of sand

and *moving* them

across the desert plateau,

making a

MOUNTAIN of SAND

that will shift and drift.

Jamal and the other animals

notice the wind, too.

Ahmed observes the effect
of the storm on his body.

He feels his robes
press against his skin.
He smells the familiar
scent of sand.
He tastes the rough dryness
of grit and tiny pebbles.
He hears the ***howl***
of the ***wind***
against his ears.

Standing alone,

Ahmed realizes his

thoughts, feelings, and emotions

are causing a storm inside his body.

He feels discomfort in his stomach

and tightness in his throat.

He realizes his thoughts

are affecting his internal world.

He notices that his
thoughts of
the upcoming race
have made him feel
anxious and fearful.

Ahmed takes a deep breath
as he has seen Jamal do many times.
He takes another breath,
deep into his belly,
and becomes curious.
What other sensations exist inside him,
and where?

Standing quietly,
Ahmed continues to observe himself.
He wonders if his internal *storm*
will move through him and depart like the
sandstorms that *pass*
across the desert.

Ahmed walks over to Jamal.
He holds Jamal's large nose and pets his soft ears.
He gazes into the animal's gentle eyes.

Ahmed feels love.

Taking another deep breath,
he feels strength in his bones
and a peacefulness settling
inside his chest and heart.

Ahmed begins to understand

the importance of taking a deep breath.

Looking around,
Ahmed notices that
the *storm* has subsided.

He checks inside his body
and notices that his internal
storm has quieted, too.
He no longer feels
small, sad, and lonely.

Instead, he feels
wise, calm, and loved.

He feels strong like the

Peaceful like the

Patient like the

Wise like the

Ahmed is grateful to be Ahmed.
He knows he has everything he needs
within himself to find peace and stillness.

Ahmed whispers a small thanks
to Jamal and the other animals,
then joins the men in the shade.

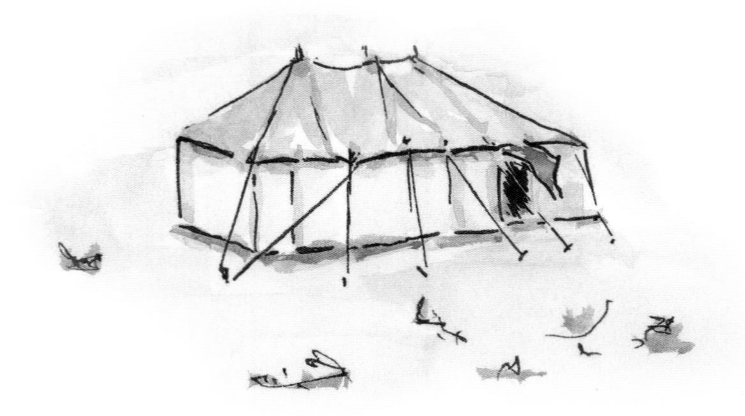

He joins the laughter
and accepts a cup of tea.

He is ready to ride Jamal
in his first camel race.

Three Meditations for Ahmed's Journey

Tea Cup

Sitting in a chair or on the ground, imagine that your body is a tea cup. Notice your breath as you gently inhale and exhale. As you take a gentle inhale, imagine your breath as tea pouring into your tea cup. Relax as you exhale and then take another gentle inhale, allowing more tea to fill your body. Take ten breaths, inhaling and exhaling at your own pace, filling your tea cup a little more with each inhale, remembering to relax on the exhale. Make sure that every little corner of your body fills up: fingers, toes, legs, arms. How does this feel in your body? It might feel different each day. Try this exercise when you wake up and also when you go to bed. Does it make you feel calm, heavy, peaceful? Which part of your body do you feel the most or the least?

Walking Exercise

Imagine that your body is still a cup of tea, but stand up and slowly walk around, stepping carefully so that you don't spill any tea. Walk slowly for about ten steps. How does it feel to walk slowly? Where are your eyes looking? How does it feel to put your feet slowly down on the Earth? Do you spill any tea? Inhale deeply to fill yourself with more tea and take long slow exhales to help you walk slowly. Don't force your breath in or out; just let it naturally come in and out of your body. Try walking up a hill, down a hill, on grass, or on sand. Remember how Ahmed watched Jamal breathe. Does paying attention to your breath help you to know how you feel inside or help to quiet your thoughts?

Tea Party

Imagine that you are sitting at a table set for a tea party with cookies and tea. Who would you like to invite to the table to join you? What would you talk about? What would you say? Pause and imagine your tea party. What kind of cookies are being served, and what does the table look like? What do you smell, see, hear, taste? How does your heart feel when you think about this tea party and about being present at this occasion with a favorite friend, family member, or animal? How does your body feel when you think about it? Notice that our thoughts can influence how we feel inside. Pause and notice how you feel inside after your imaginary tea party.

About the Author

A former overseas elementary school teacher and former Jabulani Yoga Studio owner, Jill Apperson Manly has traveled the world. She has a deep appreciation of foreign cultures and countries and enjoys blending that appreciation with her extensive knowledge of yoga to encourage children to be their true selves and to be proud of who they are. Jill is a certified iRest® teacher and Somatic Yoga Therapist. She is licensed through Yoga Alliance and received her CYT from The Chopra Center. She loves sharing yoga and meditation with children and adults, coaching girls' high school basketball, and being a mom to her four children. She lives with her husband and children in Newport Beach, CA. For more information, visit

jillamanly.com